PLANET 72

ZERO GRAVITY STATION

THIS ADVENTURE BELONGS TO:

....

....

GREEN GAS PLANET

PLANET CREAM

THE DGPH TEAM WOULD LIKE TO DEDICATE THIS BOOK TO OUR FAMILIES
AND THOSE WHO BELIEVED IN OUR DREAMS AND FANTASY WORLDS.

www.DGPH.COM.AR
www.MOLESTOWN.COM

immedium

Immedium, Inc., P.O. Box 31846, San Francisco, CA 94131
www.immedium.com

Edited by Tracy Swedlow
Design by DGPH

Printed in Singapore
10 9 8 7 6 5 4 3 2 1

Library of Congress Cataloging-in-Publication Data

DGPH (Firm)
  Space Cadet Topo : the day the sun turned off / by DGPH. -- 1st hardcover ed.
     p. cm.
  ISBN 978-1-59702-022-0 (hardcover)
  PZ7.D54133Sp 2010
  [E]--dc22

2010002434

SPACE CADET TOPO

INTERGALACTIC MOLE

THE DAY THE SUN TURNED OFF

CREATED BY DGPH

immedium

IMMEDIUM INC . SAN FRANCISCO

THIS IS SPACE CADET 3X-245, OTHERWISE KNOWN AS SPACE CADET TOPO.
TOPO IS A REALLY NICE GUY. HE CARES ABOUT EVERYONE AND ALWAYS TRIES HIS BEST.

> Telescope

> Railway Train

> Astro Radar

> Lightning ship

> Mechanical Arms

CADET TOPO WORKS AND LIVES AT THE DONUT STATION,
WHERE HE MONITORS THE UNIVERSE.

TOPO'S MULTI-FUNCTION WRISTWATCH HAS A VIDEO SCREEN, COMMUNICATOR, AND LASER BEAM – ALL THE BASIC TOOLS A CADET NEEDS.

ONE OF TOPO'S PRIMARY TASKS IS TO HELP OTHER CREATURES AND SOLVE THEIR PROBLEMS.

TOPO ALSO PICKS UP TRASH LIKE ASTEROID CRUMBS AND SATELLITE SCRAPS.
"A HEALTHY UNIVERSE IS A CLEAN ONE," SAID THE SPACE CADET.

"SOMEDAY, I WILL BECOME SPACE COMMANDER!"

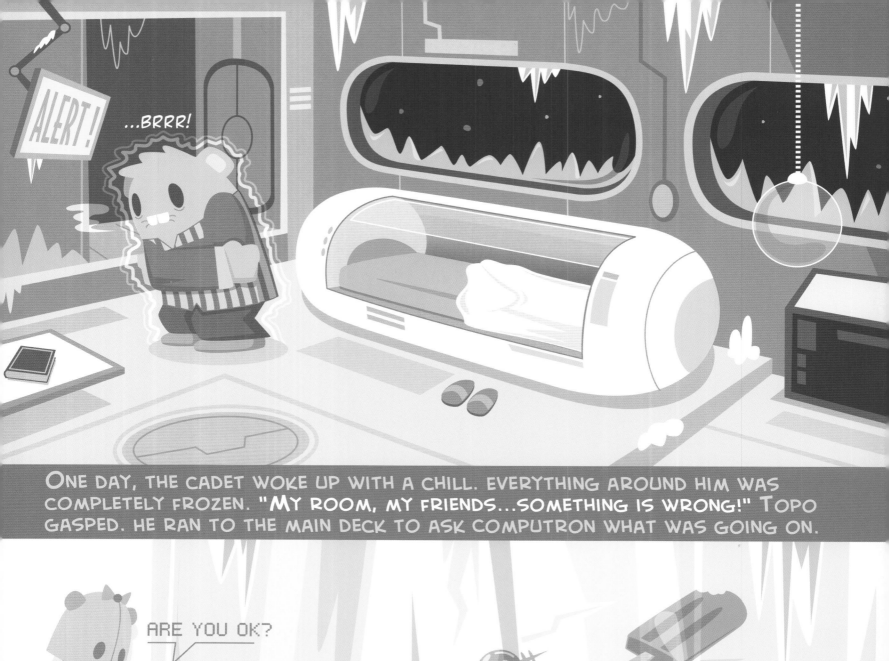

ONE DAY, THE CADET WOKE UP WITH A CHILL. EVERYTHING AROUND HIM WAS COMPLETELY FROZEN. "MY ROOM, MY FRIENDS...SOMETHING IS WRONG!" TOPO GASPED. HE RAN TO THE MAIN DECK TO ASK COMPUTRON WHAT WAS GOING ON.

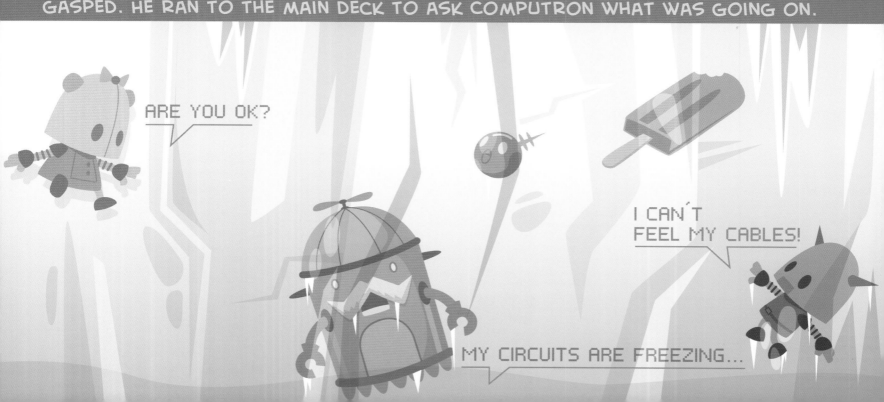

· COMPUTRON ·

EMERGENCY! EMERGENCY!

Space Cadet, the sun has turned off! The galaxy will freeze unless you fix this problem.

DONUT STATION

TASK LIST

1. Fly to the last planet in the Galaxy.
2. Find the Old Keeper of the Galactic Flame.
3. Grab the match and fly to our sun.
4. Enter the sun's core and turn the fire back on!

SUN

DANGER!

LAST PLANET IN THE GALAXY

GALACTIC FLAME MATCH

MISSION 215: TURN ON THE SUN

HANGAR PIPES

"LET'S GO, TINNY BOT! WE HAVE TO SAVE OUR FRIENDS FROM FREEZING!"

SPACE CADET TOPO RUSHED TO PREPARE FOR THE MISSION. "THE GALAXY WILL BE IN DEEP TROUBLE, IF WE CAN'T RELIGHT THE SUN IN ONE HOUR!"

IGNITION...IN 3, 2, 1...BLAST OFF!!!

LUCKILY TOPO'S LIGHTNING SHIP ZIPPED THROUGH DEEP SPACE
AT THE SPEED OF LIGHT!

On his journey, Topo saw the weather was bad and getting worse. "Every planet, moon, and star is turning blue!"

LAST PLANET IN THE GALAXY

SUN

FINALLY HE GOT TO THE LAST PLANET IN THE GALAXY. IT WAS AN OLD DUSTY ROCK IN THE MIDDLE OF NOWHERE.

LAST PLANET
IN THE GALAXY

TOPO PARKED HIS SHIP
AND WALKED DOWN THE STAIRS.

THE STEPS LED TO A BIG DARK TUNNEL FULL OF DANGER.

TRAPS LAY AT EVERY TURN.

"WE MUST COMPLETE OUR MISSION!"

TOPO REALIZED THAT SOMEONE WAS MONITORING HIM, BUT HE KEPT GOING.

OVER HERE!

AT THE END OF THE PASSAGE, TOPO FOUND A DOOR.

MEANWHILE MORE SOLAR SYSTEMS WERE GETTING COLDER.
PLANETS WERE LOOKING LIKE POPSICLES!

THE SUN SIZZLED LIKE HOT CHARCOAL
AND THE SURFACE STEAMED WITH CLOUDS OF SMOKE.

ENTRANCE

DANGER

"DONT WORRY, TINNY BOT.
I'LL PROTECT YOU," SAID TOPO.

SUDDENLY, A GREAT MONSTER EMERGED FROM THE GROUND!

BUT THE SPACE CADET WAS FASTER AND USED HIS LASER TO STUN THE BEAST.

SUN'S
CORE

TIME TO
COMPLETE MISSION
1:59 minutes

FINALLY! THEY REACHED THE SUN'S GIANT STOVE.
FOR THE FIRST TIME IN BILLIONS OF YEARS, IT SAT SILENT.
TOPO STEPPED FORWARD TO RELIGHT THE FADING FIRE ON ITS CROWN.

"GO WHILE I DISTRACT IT. YOU CAN DO IT!" URGED TOPO.

WHO? ME?!

NOW THE FATE OF THE GALAXY RESTED IN TINNY BOT'S HANDS.

TIME TO
COMPLETE MISSION
0:24 seconds

LUCKILY, SHE REMEMBERED THE TICKING CLOCK. THEY ONLY HAD SECONDS LEFT.
TINNY BOT FORGOT HER FEARS AND RACED TO THE TOP OF THE MACHINE.

AFTER RETURNING THE GALACTIC FLAME TO ITS RIGHTFUL HOME, THE CADET AND HIS PAL FLEW BACK TO THE STATION.

THEY LOOKED FORWARD TO DEFROSTING THEIR FRIENDS AND WATCHING THE GALAXY GET BACK TO NORMAL.

UNTIL THE NEXT MISSION, SPACE CADET TOPO!

END OF TRANSMISSION_

◢UFOs

◢SUN

◢BLUE COMET

◢EMPTY ASTEROID

◢WEATHER SATELLITE